# Just in Time for Christmas

BY
## LOUISE BORDEN

ILLUSTRATED BY
## TED LEWIN

Scholastic Inc.
New York

To all the teachers and librarians who have welcomed me to their classrooms and their schools . . . especially Mrs. Kroeger, Mrs. Homon, Mrs. Carter, and Mrs. Dodd.
—L.B.

To the gang at the farm.
—T.L.

Copyright © 1994 by Louise W. Borden.  Illustrations copyright © 1994 by Ted Lewin.
All rights reserved. Published by Scholastic Inc.
SCHOLASTIC HARDCOVER is a registered trademark of Scholastic Inc.

No part of this publication may be reproduced in whole or in part, or stored in a retrieval system,
or transmitted in any form or by any means, electronic, mechanical, photocopying,
recording, or otherwise, without written permission of the publisher.
For information regarding permission, write to Scholastic Inc., 555 Broadway, New York, NY 10012.
*Library of Congress Cataloging-in-Publication Data*
Borden, Louise.
Just in time for Christmas / by Louise Borden; illustrated by Ted Lewin.
p.    cm.
Summary: A young boy, living in rural Kentucky, looks forward to the annual Christmas festivities,
especially the traditional family cream candy: but, when his favorite dog disappears,
he comes to realize that tradition and family have a deeper meaning.
ISBN 0-590-45355-6
[1. Christmas—Fiction. 2. Family life—Fiction. 3. Dogs—Fiction.
4. Country life—Kentucky—Fiction. 5. Kentucky—Fiction.]
I. Lewin, Ted, ill. II. Title. PZ7.B64827Ju   1994
[E]—dc20  93-40082    CIP  AC
12  11  10  9  8  7  6  5  4  3  2  1     4  5  6  7  8  9/9
Printed in the U.S.A.                    37
First printing, October 1994
Book design by Kristina Iulo
Mr. Lewin used watercolor paints to create
the illustrations for this book.

Special thanks to our good friends and their children
who came to the farm and helped make this book.
—L.B.

It seems like such a long time to wait,
going all year without a piece of cream candy.

My friend Chandler says our candy
will be the best Christmas present coming.
He says everyone must be waiting for the Bryans
to start making candy.
Even my dog Luke,
who has the sweetest tooth around.

"Bryans have been pulling candy on this porch
for over a hundred years . . ."

That's what my great-grandmother tells
Chandler and me.
Great Gram stands on the porch with Luke
and remembers Christmases that we cannot.
Even though she forgets my name.
Even though she calls me Charlie.
Or Joe.

I help my brothers feed the dogs just before dark.
Luke and Traverse are the best hunting dogs in the valley.
Luke's my favorite because he's his own boss.

Charlie rubs Traverse behind the ears and asks,
"Is it cream candy time yet?"
And I shake my head no,
and say that I am waiting, too.

I tell Charlie and Joe about the hundred years of candy.
I tell them a hundred years of candy
would fill the tobacco barn beyond the creek.

We wait past November for cream candy weather,
when the Kentucky air is hard and clear.
The sycamore logs echo with a cold thunk
when Joe and I bring in firewood from the porch.
I try to let Luke in, but my mother says no.

I see him head past the creek . . .
and he's off chasing squirrels.

He doesn't come home for dinner that night,
or the night after that.
"He's just being his own boss," says my father.

I worry about Luke.
He's been gone two days.
After school, Chandler and I whistle for him,
but he doesn't come home.
We call up the neighbors.
No one's seen my dog.

"He'll come home for Christmas," says Great Gram.
"All the Bryans do . . ."

Our cousins come with suitcases,
from Delaware, miles away.
Our house is filled with my mother's sisters
and all the stories that they share.
Great Gram thinks my cousin Nick is me,
and she calls him Will.

And then our grandmother Punch arrives.
Punch, with her strong wide hands,
loves dogs, just like me.

I tell everyone about Luke.
I tell everyone I don't even care about Christmas this year.

Great Gram pats my hand and says:
"He'll be back in time for Christmas . . ."
I figure she's right.
But then she calls me Joe.

It is a cold time,
and a family time.
It's a Bryan time,
and the waiting is over!

My uncles bring in the fir tree,
one we cut from the north field.

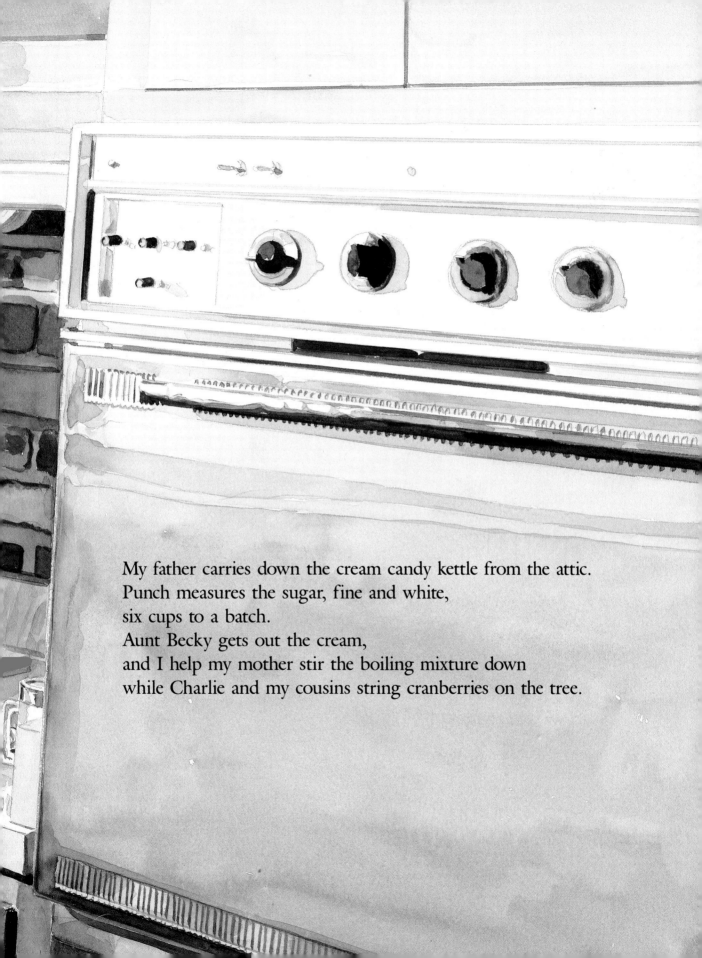

My father carries down the cream candy kettle from the attic.
Punch measures the sugar, fine and white,
six cups to a batch.
Aunt Becky gets out the cream,
and I help my mother stir the boiling mixture down
while Charlie and my cousins string cranberries on the tree.

I worry about Luke.
He's been gone five days.
Maybe he's in trouble somewhere,
up in our woods.
Punch and I go out across the fields
to call for my dog.
We shout his name loud,
and it echoes off the hills.

I let Traverse in,
quiet like,
and he curls up behind the chair.
My father bangs out carols on the old black piano.
Our singing helps the time pass
while the mixture boils and foams.
The whole house smells of our candy,
of sugar,
and vanilla,
and cream.
It is the smell of Christmas, every year.
Every year for a hundred years.

And then . . .

"The candy's turning color!" calls my mother.
And so it is.
The boiling bubbles are as pale as ginger ale.
I hang over my father's shoulder as he lifts the heavy kettle.
Everyone follows him out to the porch.
I shoo Traverse away while the candy's poured
onto the cold marble slab.
We stand on the porch,
every Bryan,
from Great Gram and Punch,
all the way down to me.

Everyone gets a turn at the pulling.
My father has the best pulling hands.
The candy doesn't stick to them like mine,
and I watch him twist and turn the long thick rope of taffy.
It gleams in the air like Christmas snow.

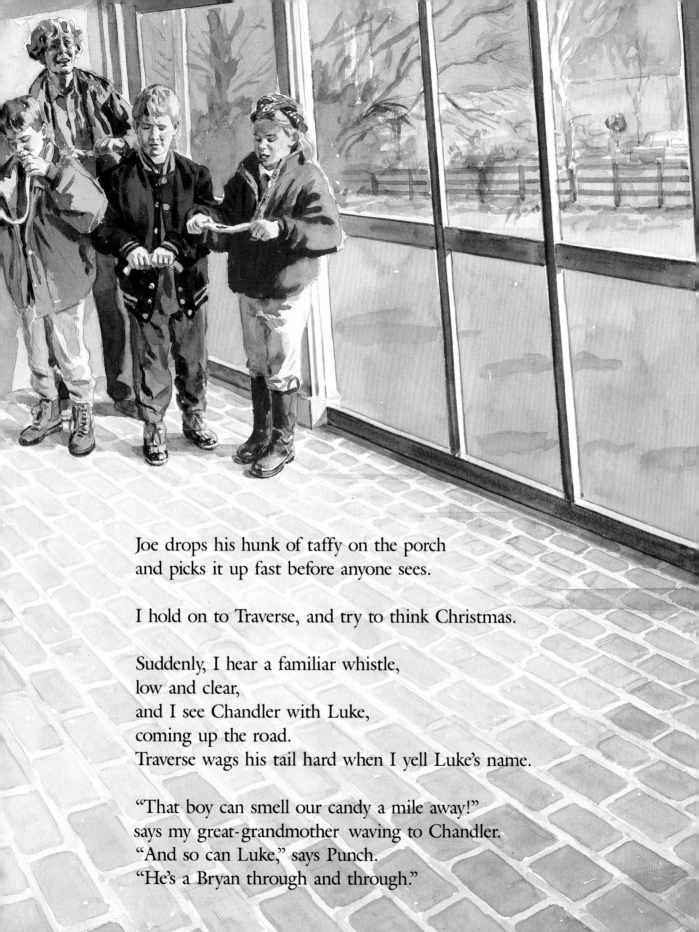

Joe drops his hunk of taffy on the porch
and picks it up fast before anyone sees.

I hold on to Traverse, and try to think Christmas.

Suddenly, I hear a familiar whistle,
low and clear,
and I see Chandler with Luke,
coming up the road.
Traverse wags his tail hard when I yell Luke's name.

"That boy can smell our candy a mile away!"
says my great-grandmother waving to Chandler.
"And so can Luke," says Punch.
"He's a Bryan through and through."

We stay on the porch in our coats,
with red cheeks and cold hands.
Everyone gets a turn at cutting
the long sweet ropes into pieces, fat and square.
We each grab a piece,
and the waiting is behind us,
stretched out long like a train full of days.
I sneak Luke a lick of candy.
The candy begins to cream:
It turns from chewing gum soft to butter mint hard.
"I like it soft best," I tell Chandler.
"So do I," says Great Gram,
and she calls me Will.

Later,
my mother shoos the dogs off the porch
and sends all the cousins
to hang a wreath on the barn beyond the creek.
We sit in the hay,
smelling seasons of tobacco,
and eating cream candy till our teeth ache.

The dogs curl up beside us,
and Chandler tells me again
how he found Luke chasing quail.
It begins to snow,
just in time for Christmas.